MEET THE CHARACTERS

BEN TENNYSON
TEN TIMES MORE TROUBLE THAN THE AVERAGE KID!

GWEN TENNYSON
RED-HEADED VOICE OF REASON TO HER COUSIN BEN

GRANDPA MAX
JUST A MILD-MANNERED GRANDFATHER – OR IS HE?...

VILGAX
ALIEN WARLORD WITH A REAL ATTITUDE PROBLEM

FOUR ARMS
PROOF THAT FOUR ARMS ARE BETTER THAN TWO

HEATBLAST
THIS ALIEN'S ON FIRE!

STINKFLY
THERE'S NO FLY SWAT BIG ENOUGH FOR THIS INSECT

DIAMONDHEAD
YOU COULD SAY HE'S A SHARP SHOOTER

UPGRADE
NEVER HAS A PROBLEM WTH MODERN TECHNOLOGY...

GHOSTFREAK
YOU WON'T FIND HIM BEATING HIS HEAD AGAINST BRICK WALLS

GREY MATTER
HE'S A CLEVER LITTLE THING

WILDMUTT
HE'S ONE DOGGIE YOU SHOULDN'T PET!

RIPJAWS
NEVER BITES OFF MORE THAN HE CAN CHEW

XLR8
HE'S ALWAYS UP TO SPEED

EGMONT

We bring stories to life

First published in Great Britain 2010 by Dean,
an imprint of Egmont UK Limited,
239 Kensington High Street, London W8 6SA
All Rights Reserved

ISBN 978 0 6035 6513 7
3 5 7 9 10 8 6 4 2
Printed and bound in Italy

AND THEN THERE WERE 10

AND THEN THERE WERE 10

BEN TENNYSON IS A 10-YEAR-OLD KID WHO'S JUST FINISHED SCHOOL FOR THE SUMMER. HE'S OFF ON A ROAD TRIP WITH HIS GRANDPA MAX IN THEIR OLD 'RV' – THE RUSTBUCKET! MEANWHILE, STRANGE THINGS ARE HAPPENING IN OUTER SPACE.

AN ALIEN SPACESHIP IS CRUISING SILENTLY THROUGH SPACE WHEN SUDDENLY, *BOOM!* A SMALLER SHIP DELIVERS A DEVASTATING BLAST OF ENERGY!
ZAP! POW! THE ATTACK CONTINUES, ROCKING THE BIGGER SPACE CRAFT.
POW!
ON BOARD THE DAMAGED SHIP IS THE MONSTROUS-LOOKING VILGAX, AN EVIL ALIEN WARLORD.
ZAP!
I HAVE COME TOO FAR TO BE DENIED.
THE OMNITRIX SHALL BE MINE, AND THERE IS NOT A BEING IN THE GALAXY WHO DARES STAND IN MY WAY!
THE SPACE CHASE CONTINUES ...

MEANWHILE, ON PLANET EARTH, BEN TENNYSON IS GETTING UP TO HIS USUAL PRANKS IN THE CLASSROOM. IT'S THE LAST DAY OF THE SCHOOL YEAR, AND HE CAN'T WAIT TO GET AWAY. THE CLOCK TURNS THREE.

YES! OUTTA HERE!

BEN'S HEADING OUT THE DOOR.

OUTSIDE, BEN'S GRANDPA MAX IS WAITING IN HIS RV.

COME ON BEN, LET'S GO.

WE'RE BURNING DAYLIGHT. I WANT TO MAKE IT TO THE CAMPSITE BY NIGHTFALL.

BEN CLIMBS ON BOARD THE RV. BUT HE IS IN FOR A SHOCK!

WHAT IS **SHE** DOING HERE?

IT'S HIS COUSIN, GWEN.

TAKE IT EASY DWEEB, THIS WASN'T MY IDEA. SOMEONE CONVINCED MY MUM THAT GOING CAMPING FOR THE SUMMER WOULD BE GOOD FOR ME.

I THOUGHT IT WOULD BE FUN IF YOUR COUSIN JOINED US THIS SUMMER, IS THAT A PROBLEM?

"I CAN'T BELIEVE IT, I WAIT ALL SCHOOL YEAR TO GO ON THIS TRIP, AND NOW THE QUEEN OF COOTIES IS ALONG FOR THE RIDE!" MOANS BEN.

IT'S ALMOST DARK BY THE TIME THEY GET TO THE CAMPSITE. MAX QUICKLY FIXES UP SOME DINNER.

"CHOW TIME!" SAYS MAX. "MARINATED MEAL WORMS. IT'S HARD TO FIND THEM FRESH. THEY'RE A DELICACY IN SOME COUNTRIES."

AND TOTALLY GROSS IN OTHERS!

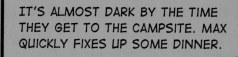

URGH, COULDN'T WE JUST HAVE A BURGER OR SOMETHING?

"IF THESE DON'T SOUND GOOD," CONTINUES MAX, "I'VE GOT SOME SMOKED SHEEP'S TONGUE IN THE FRIDGE ..."

"LOOKS LIKE A SATELLITE OR SOMETHING," THINKS BEN, LOOKING AT THE OBJECT

THE GROUND GIVES WAY, AND BEN FALLS INTO THE HOLE! THE OBJECT SPLITS OPEN TO REVEAL A WEIRD-LOOKING WATCH, GLOWING BRIGHT GREEN.

A WATCH. WHAT'S A WATCH DOING IN OUTER SPACE?

BEN REACHES FOR THE WATCH AND *WHOOSH!* IT JUMPS ON TO HIS LEFT WRIST - AND LOCKS TIGHT!

AGGGH!!

GET OFF ME, GET OFF, *GET OFF!* *GRANDPA* ...

BEN RUNS ALL OVER THE PLACE, SHOUTING AND SCREAMING.

BACK IN THE FOREST, BEN PULLS HIMSELF OUT OF THE CRATER. HE TRIES AGAIN TO GET THE WATCH OFF, BUT NOTHING WORKS.

BEN TAKES A CLOSE LOOK AT THE WATCH AND PRESSES A BUTTON. IT POPS UP AND BLINKS GREEN. A PICTURE OF A MONSTER SUDDENLY APPEARS.

COOL!

BEN CAN'T RESIST PRESSING THE BUTTON.

... AND SUDDENLY BEN HAS TRANSFORMED INTO A BURNING MAN – *HEATBLAST!* HE RUNS THROUGH THE FOREST CRYING OUT IN TERROR.

AGGGH!

I'M ON FIRE, I'M ON FIRE ... HEY, I'M ON FIRE, AND I'M OK. CHECK IT OUT,

I'M TOTALLY HOT!

BEN TRIES OUT HIS NEW POWERS – IT'S PRETTY COOL BEING ABLE TO SHOOT *FIREBALLS!* BUT IT ISN'T LONG BEFORE HE ACCIDENTALLY SETS FIRE TO SOME TREES. THE FIRE SPREADS AND SOON A HUGE FOREST FIRE IS RAGING! HEATBLAST PANICS.

JUST THEN, MAX AND GWEN APPEAR, ARMED WITH FIRE EXTINGUISHERS. BUT THEY DIDN'T RECKON ON FINDING BEN DISGUISED AS A MONSTER FIREBALL!

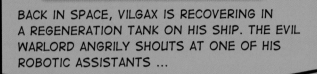

BACK IN SPACE, VILGAX IS RECOVERING IN A REGENERATION TANK ON HIS SHIP. THE EVIL WARLORD ANGRILY SHOUTS AT ONE OF HIS ROBOTIC ASSISTANTS ...

WHAT DO YOU MEAN IT'S NOT THERE? THIS BATTLE NEARLY COSTS ME MY LIFE AND YOU SAY THE OMNITRIX IS NO LONGER ON BOARD?

THE ROBOT REPORTS THAT "SENSORS INDICATE A PROBE WAS JETTISONED FROM THE SHIP JUST BEFORE BOARDING. IT LANDED ON THE PLANET BELOW."

GO!
BRING IT TO ME!

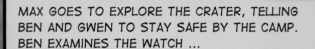

MAX GOES TO EXPLORE THE CRATER, TELLING BEN AND GWEN TO STAY SAFE BY THE CAMP. BEN EXAMINES THE WATCH ...

"SO," SAYS GWEN, "WHAT DID IT FEEL LIKE GOING ALL ALIEN?"

IT FREAKED ME OUT AT FIRST. HEY, I THINK I FIGURED OUT HOW I DID IT. SHOULD I TRY IT AGAIN, JUST ONCE?

BEN PRESSES THE WATCH ... AND TRANSFORMS INTO A WILD-LOOKING, HAIRY, GROWLING, DROOLING BEAST. IT'S *WILDMUTT!*

"YEUGH!" SAYS GWEN. "THIS THING'S EVEN UGLIER THAN YOU ARE NORMALLY! YOU NEED A FLEA COLLAR ON THIS MUTT! AND NO EYES? WHAT GOOD IS THIS ONE? IT CAN'T SEE!"

WILDMUTT MAY NOT HAVE EYES, BUT HIS RADAR-LIKE 'VISION' CAN DETECT PEOPLE AND OBJECTS AROUND HIM. HE BOUNDS OFF INTO THE FOREST, LEAPING AND SWINGING FROM TREE TO TREE ...

BEFORE LONG, WILDMUTT SENSES DANGER. A ROBOTIC DRONE FLIES TOWARDS HIM!

WILDMUTT JUMPS ON TOP OF THE DRONE. WITH HIS SHARP TEETH HE TEARS ITS WIRES OUT, AND THE DRONE SPINS WILDLY OUT OF CONTROL! WILDMUTT LEAPS OFF, SECONDS BEFORE THE MACHINE EXPLODES.

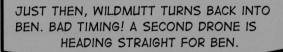

JUST THEN, WILDMUTT TURNS BACK INTO BEN. BAD TIMING! A SECOND DRONE IS HEADING STRAIGHT FOR BEN.

LUCKILY GWEN ARRIVES, AND SHE SMACKS THE DRONE HARD WITH A SPADE, AND DESTROYS IT. BEN IS IMPRESSED!

NEVER THOUGHT I'D SAY THIS, BUT AM I GLAD TO SEE YOU!

BEN AND GWEN RUN BACK TO THE CAMP TO FIND GRANDPA MAX.

BACK AT CAMP, THE TEAM HEAR A MAYDAY CALL OVER THE RUSTBUCKET'S RADIO – "MAYDAY, MAYDAY! SOMEBODY HELP US. WE'RE UNDER ATTACK BY SOME SORT OF ... ROBOT!"
SOUNDS JUST LIKE THOSE THINGS THAT ATTACKED ME, THEY MUST BE LOOKING FOR THE WATCH. I THINK I CAN HELP!
WITH A PRESS OF THE BUTTON, BEN TRANSFORMS ONCE AGAIN, THIS TIME INTO A MAN TOUGHER THAN ANY METAL. IT'S *DIAMONDHEAD!*
"SO," SAYS GWEN, "WHAT CAN THIS GUY DO?"
I DUNNO, BUT I BET IT'S GONNA BE COOL!

DIAMONDHEAD, MAX AND GWEN ARRIVE AT THE SCENE OF THE ATTACK. VILGAX'S HUGE ROBOTIC ASSISTANT HAS LANDED ON EARTH TO CAPTURE THE OMNITRIX. HE'S FIRING WEAPONS, CAUSING EXPLOSIONS AND FIRES. CAMPERS ARE RUNNING FOR THEIR LIVES ...

"LOOKS LIKE PAPA ROBOT THIS TIME," SAYS DIAMONDHEAD. "I'LL GET GEARHEAD'S ATTENTION. YOU TWO GUYS GET THE CAMPERS TO SAFETY."

THE ROBOT IS FIERCE, BUT DIAMONDHEAD'S GLASS-LIKE SURFACE REFLECTS ITS LASERS BACK AT IT. FINALLY, THE ROBOT RIVAL IS DESTROYED!

BACK ON HIS SPACESHIP, THE INJURED VILGAX CANNOT BELIEVE THAT HIS DRONE HAS FAILED TO GET THE OMNITRIX.

AT THE CAMPSITE, MAX AND GWEN ARE PACKING UP, GETTING READY TO LEAVE. SUDDENLY A SUPER-SPEEDY ALIEN APPEARS. IT'S BEN AS XLR8! HE ZIPS AROUND AND HELPS PACK UP THE RUSTBUCKET. HE'S SO FAST!

NO!

"I THINK THIS IS GOING TO BE THE BEST SUMMER EVER!" LAUGHS XLR8.

"ABSOLUTELY!" AGREES MAX.

"IT'S DEFINITELY GOING TO BE INTERESTING ..." SAYS GWEN.